FAMILY PETS

OUR PET TURTLE

by Michele Jakubowski
illustrated by Kev Payne

GRASSHOPPER

Tools for Parents & Teachers

Grasshopper Books enhance imagination and introduce the earliest readers to fiction with fun storylines and illustrations. The easy-to-read text supports early reading experiences with repetitive sentence patterns and sight words.

Before Reading

- Look at the cover illustration. What do readers see? What do they think the book will be about?
- Look at the picture glossary together. Sound out the words. Ask readers to identify the first letter of each vocabulary word.

Read the Book

- "Walk" through the book, reading to or along with the reader. Point to the illustrations as you read.

After Reading

- Review the picture glossary again. Ask readers to locate the words in the text.
- Ask the reader: Shelly the turtle is a reptile. What other kinds of reptiles do you know of? What makes them reptiles?

Grasshopper Books are published by Jump!
5357 Penn Avenue South
Minneapolis, MN 55419
www.jumplibrary.com

Library of Congress Cataloging-in-Publication Data

Names: Jakubowski, Michele, author. | Payne, Kev, 1978- illustrator.
Title: Our pet turtle / by Michele Jakubowski; illustrated by Kev Payne.
Description: Minneapolis, MN: Jump!, Inc., [2022]
Series: Family pets
Includes reading tips and supplementary back matter.
Audience: Ages 5-7.
Identifiers: LCCN 2020058541 (print)
LCCN 2020058542 (ebook)
ISBN 9781636902074 (hardcover)
ISBN 9781636902081 (paperback)
ISBN 9781636902098 (ebook)
Subjects: LCSH: Readers (Primary)
Turtles as pets–Juvenile fiction.
Classification: LCC PE1119.2 .J356 2022 (print)
LCC PE1119.2 (ebook)
DDC 428.6/2–dc23
LC record available at https://lccn.loc.gov/2020058541
LC ebook record available at https://lccn.loc.gov/2020058542

Editor: Eliza Leahy
Direction and Layout: Anna Potorson
Illustrator: Kev Payne

Printed in the United States of America at Corporate Graphics in North Mankato, Minnesota.

Table of Contents

Taking Care of Shelly

This is Shelly!
She is our class turtle.

I get to take Shelly home over spring break.

"Don't forget Shelly's food, Sam!" says my teacher.

At home, we set up
Shelly's tank.

We put fresh water in.
We make sure it is warm.

Shelly is a reptile.
She needs heat.

75°F

Shelly climbs on her rock.

She stands under her heat lamp.

Shelly swims!

I watch her webbed feet.

I feed Shelly each day.

Kale is a treat!

I pick Shelly up.
I use two hands.

She walks on my hands.
She is slow. It tickles!

I wash my hands
after holding her.

At night, I turn off Shelly's lamp.

"Good night, Shelly!" I say.

Let's Review!

What does Sam do after holding Shelly?

A. eats a snack **B.** washes his hands
C. watches TV **D.** takes a nap

Picture Glossary

kale
A leafy vegetable with green or purple leaves.

reptile
A cold-blooded animal that crawls or creeps on short legs.

tank
A container in which fish and other water animals and plants can live.

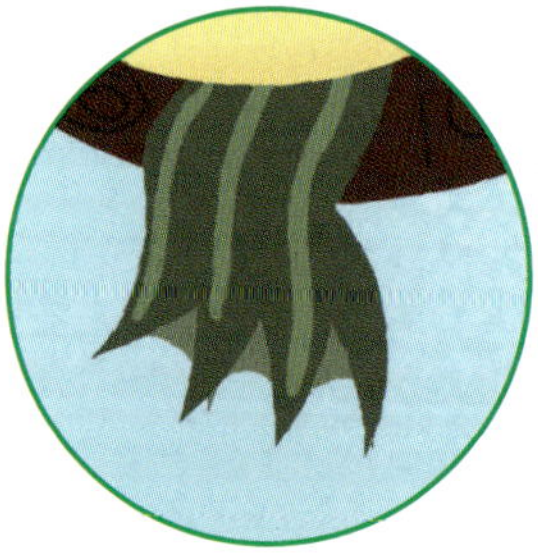

webbed
Having the digits, such as toes, joined by tissue.

Let's Review! Answer Key: **B.** washes his hands